FOR ELYSSA, ALEXA, and ROMELLE

VOYEUR

JEFF DUNAS
VOYEUR

MELROSE

Also by the same author:
MADEMOISELLE, MADEMOISELLE!
CAPTURED WOMEN

Copyright © J.R.D. Photography, Inc. 1983. All rights reserved under International and Pan-American Copyright Conventions. No part of this publication may be reproduced, stored in a retrieval system or transmitted, in any form or by any means, electronic, mechanical, photocopying, recording or otherwise, without the express prior written permission of the author and publisher, except for the purpose of a review written for inclusion in a magazine, newspaper or broadcast. Any photograph or excerpt reproduced for review must include copyright notice as it appears above. Second printing. First published in 1983. I.S.B.N. 0-394-53348-8. Library of Congress Catalogue number 83-48405. Published by Melrose Publishing Company, Inc. 9021 Melrose Avenue, Suite 301, Los Angeles, California 90069. Distributed in the United States and Canada by Grove Press, Inc. 196 West Houston Street, New York, N.Y. 10014. Manufactured in France.

JEFF DUNAS has done it again.

His first two albums "Captured Women" in 1981, and "Mademoiselle, Mademoiselle!" in 1982 were enthusiastically received. "Voyeur", a suggestive and unusual title, is more an exemplary gallery of portraits than a simple collection of photographs. I have the presentiment that I am writing about the latest creation of a great artist, although what I have to say is of little consequence. It is the photographs which are important, veritable "chef d'œuvres" in my estimation.

"The perfection of art", wrote Quintillion, the great rhetor-poet of the first century A.D., "is when the art is not apparent". This elequently describes what is, perhaps, the secret of his success. With an alert intelligence and a mastery of technique, Jeff Dunas achieves a fluency in that marvelous language of man, that of photography. His shadows dance in remarkably geometric compositions enhanced by a unique and poetic use of light.

He loves women, this we feel and see. I would even say he adores them. They are his obsession, his passion and his need. His eye, surprisingly precise, imortalizes women in images that become erotic poetry, sources of fantasy.

The voyeur, Jeff Dunas, makes of us his accomplices. This is why I believe you will find your senses awakened, your sense of beauty enriched as you pause before each tableau.

Dieu que l'art est noble lorsque la tête, le cœur et la main travaillent ensemble!
(Heavens, art is noble when the head, the heart and the hand work together!)

Roger Borniche
Paris, 1983

THINGS move to Power and Beauty; I say that much and I have said all that I can say.

But what is Beauty, you ask, and what will Power do? And here I reach my utmost point in the direction of what you are free to call the rhapsodical and the incomprehensible. I will not even attempt to define Beauty. I will not because I cannot. To me it is a final, quite indefinable thing. Either you understand it or you do not. Every true artist and many who are not artists know — they know there is something that shows suddenly — it may be in music, it may be in painting, it may be in the sunlight on a glacier or shadows cast by a furnace or the scent of a flower; it may be in the person or act of some fellow creature, but it is right, it is commanding, it is, to use theological language, the revelation of God.

To the mystery of Power and Beauty, out of the earth that mothered us, we move. I do not attempt to define Beauty nor even to distinguish it from Power. I do not think indeed that one can effectually distinguish these aspects of life. I do not know how far Beauty may not be simple fullness and clearness of sensation, a momentary unveiling of things hitherto seen but not dully and darkly. As I have already said there may be beauty in the feeling of beer in the throat, in the taste of cheese in the mouth, there may be beauty in the scent of earth, in the warmth of a body, in the sensation of waking from sleep. I use the word Beauty therefore in its widest possible sense, ranging far beyond the special beauties that art discovers and develops. Perhaps as we pass from death to life all things become beautiful. The utmost I can do in conveying what I mean by Beauty is to tell of things that I have perceived to be beautiful as beautifully as I can tell of them. It may be, as I suggest elsewhere, Beauty is a thing synthetic and not simple; it is a common effect produced by a great medley of causes, a larger aspect of harmony.

But the question of what Beauty is does not very gready concern me, since I have known it when I met it and almost every day in life I seem to apprehend it more and to find it more sufficient and satisfying. It is light. I fall back upon that image, it is all things that light can be, beacon, eludidation, pleasure, comfort and consolation, promise, warning, the vision of reality.

H. G. WELLS *(From "First and Last Things", 1909)*

Rambouillet, France 1979

Les Essarts-le-Roi, France 1982

Les Essarts-le-Roi, France 1982

Les Essarts-le-Roi, France 1982

Welwyn Garden City, England 1982

Welwyn Garden City, England 1982

Melun, France 1980

Paris, France 1982

Paris, France 1982

Welwyn Garden City, England 1982

Welwyn Garden City, England 1982

Passy, France 1983

Hertfordshire, England 1982

Hertfordshire, England 1982

Nemours, France 1983

Nemours, France 1983

Los Angeles, California 1983

Los Angeles, California 1982

Paris, France 1982

Paris, France 1982

Pasadena, California 1983

Les Essarts-le-Roi, France 1982

Les Essarts-le-Roi, France 1982

La Chapelle, Normandie, France 1981

Northiam, East Sussex, England 1982

Northiam, East Sussex, England 1982

Bussy le Repos, France 1983

Bussy le Repos, France 1983

Welwyn Garden City, England 1982

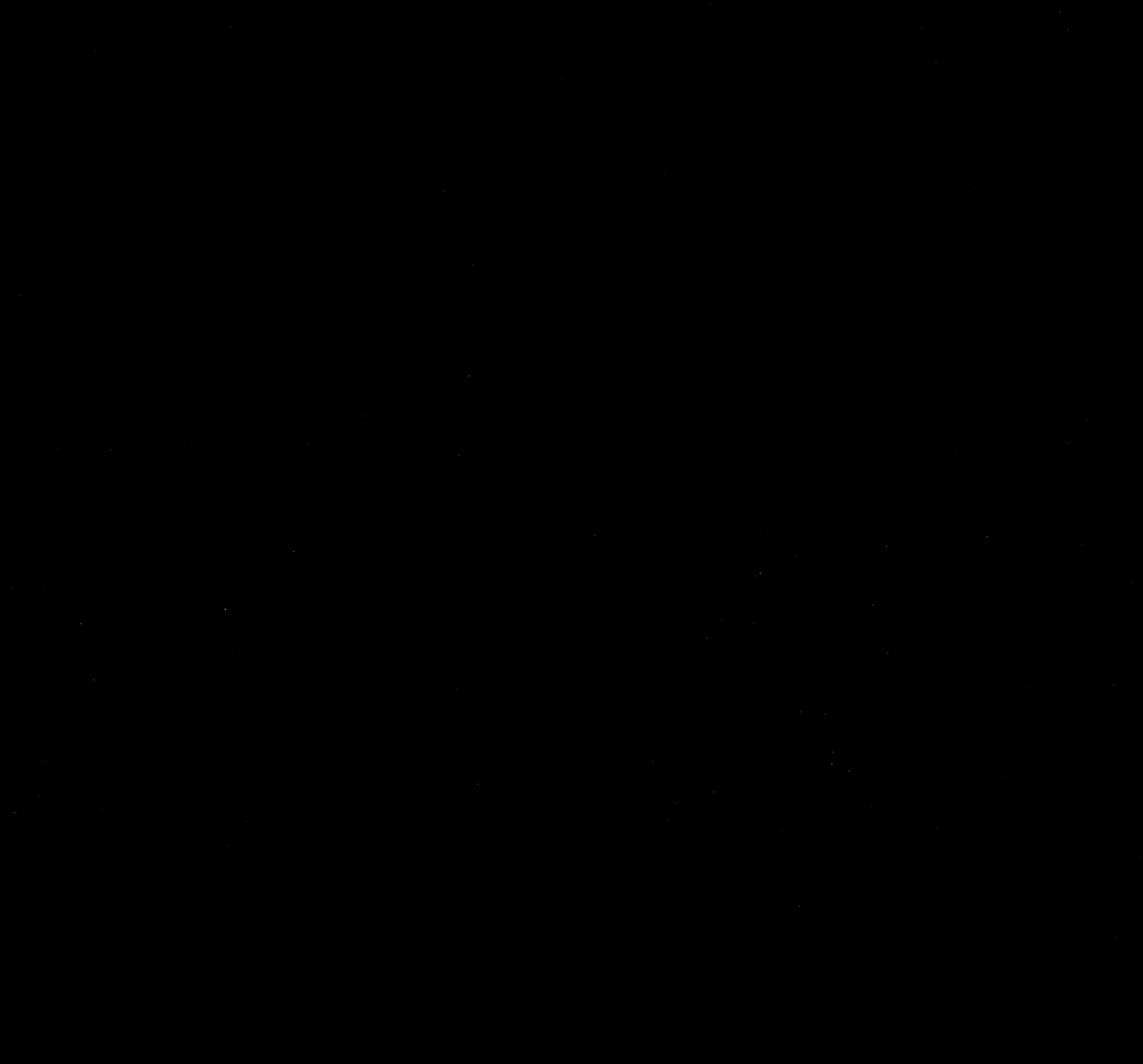

Epernon, France 1983

Droue-s-Drouette, France 1982

Malibu, California 1983

Pasadena, California 1983

Bussy le Repos, France 1983

Bussy le Repos, France 1983

Bussy le Repos, France 1983

Bussy le Repos, France 1983

Nemours, France 1983

Nemours, France 1983

Los Angeles, California 1983

Los Angeles, California 1983

Beverly Hills, California 1983

Hollywood, California 1982

Los Angeles, California 1982

Long Island, New York 1980

Long Island, New York 1980

Rambouillet, France
August 1979
Daylight, 105 mm lens
Kodachrome-64

La Sartrelle,
Les Essarts-le-Roi, France, I
May 1982
Daylight, 200 mm lens
Kodachrome-64

La Sartrelle,
Les Essarts-le-Roi, France, II
May 1982
Daylight, 200 mm lens
Kodachrome-64

La Sartrelle,
Les Essarts-le-Roi, France, III
May 1982
Daylight, 35 mm lens
Kodachrome-64

Welwyn Garden City,
Hertfordshire, England, I
August 1982
Daylight, 24 mm lens
Kodachrome-25

Welwyn Garden City,
Hertfordshire, England, II
August 1982
Daylight, 24 mm lens
Kodachrome-25

Grayhall Mansion,
Beverly Hills, California, I
January 1983
Flash, 24 mm lens
Kodachrome-64

Grayhall Mansion,
Beverly Hills, California, II
January 1983
Flash, 85 mm lens
Kodachrome-64

Melun, France
November 1980
Daylight, Flash, 35 mm lens
Kodachrome-64

Paris, France, I
May 1982
Daylight, Flash, 105 mm lens
Kodachrome-64

Paris, France, II
May 1982
Daylight, Flash, 105 mm lens
Kodachrome-64

Brocket Hall, Welwyn Garden City,
Hertfordshire, England, I
August 1982
Flash, 24 mm lens
Kodachrome-64

Brocket Hall, Welwyn Garden City,
Hertfordshire, England, II
August 1982
Flash, 24 mm lens
Kodachrome-64

Brocket Hall, Welwyn Garden City,
Hertfordshire, England, III
August 1982
Daylight, 35 mm lens
Kodachrome-64

Passy, France
July 1983
Daylight, Flash
24 mm lens
Kodachrome-64

Brocket Hall, Welwyn Garden City, IV
Hertfordshire, England, IV
August 1982
Daylight, Flash, 24 mm lens
Kodachrome-64

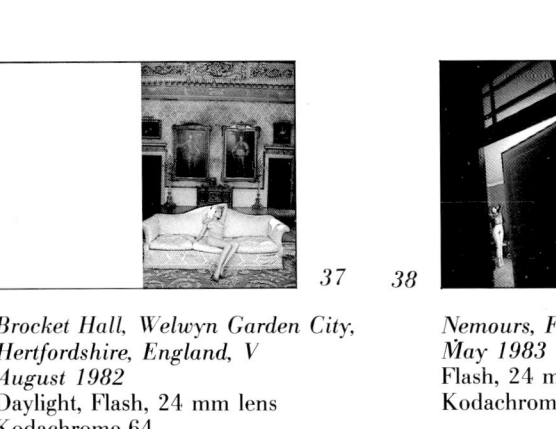

37
*Brocket Hall, Welwyn Garden City,
Hertfordshire, England, V*
August 1982
Daylight, Flash, 24 mm lens
Kodachrome-64

38
Nemours, France, I
May 1983
Flash, 24 mm lens
Kodachrome-64

39
Nemours, France, II
May 1983
Flash, 24 mm lens
Kodachrome-64

41
*Los Angeles,
California*
February 1983
Daylight, 180 mm lens
Kodachrome-64

43
*Los Angeles,
California*
February 1982
Flash, 35 mm lens
Kodachrome-25

44
*Hôtel de Crillon,
Paris, France, I*
November 1982
Daylight, Flash, 35 mm lens
Kodachrome-64

45
*Hôtel de Crillon,
Paris, France, II*
November 1982
Daylight, Flash, 28 mm lens
Kodachrome-64

47
*Los Angeles,
California*
January 1983
Daylight, Flash, 180 mm lens
Kodachrome-64

49
*Pasadena,
California*
January 1983
Daylight, 35 mm lens
Kodachrome-25

50
*La Sartrelle,
Les Essarts-le-Roi, France, IV*
May 1982
Daylight, Flash, 24 mm lens
Kodachrome-64

51
*La Sartrelle,
Les Essarts-le-Roi, France, V*
May 1982
Daylight, Flash, 24 mm lens
Kodachrome-64

53
*La Chapelle,
Normandie, France*
April 1981
Daylight, 300 mm lens
Kodachrome-25

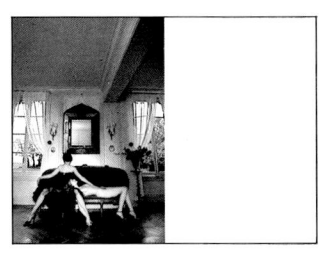

55
*Northiam,
East Sussex, England, I*
August 1982
Daylight, 135 mm lens
Kodachrome-64

57
*Northiam,
East Sussex, England, II*
August 1982
Daylight, Flash, 20 mm lens
Kodachrome-64

58
*Les Jolis Vaux,
Bussy le Repos, France, I*
May 1983
Daylight, Flash, 24 mm lens
Kodachrome-64

59
*Les Jolis Vaux,
Bussy le Repos, France, II*
May 1983
Daylight, Flash, 24 mm lens
Kodachrome-64

60

*Brocket Hall, Welwyn Garden City,
Hertfordshire, England, VI
August 1982*
Daylight, Flash, 24 mm lens
Kodachrome-64

61

*Brocket Hall, Welwyn Garden City,
Hertfordshire, England, VII
August 1982*
Daylight, Flash, 24 mm lens
Kodachrome-64

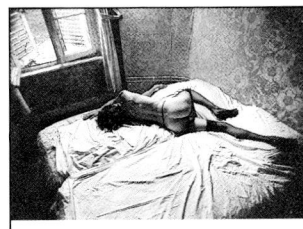

63

*Les Jolis Vaux,
Bussy le Repos, France, III
May 1983*
Daylight, Flash, 35 mm lens
Kodachrome-64

64

*Epernon, France
April 1983*
Daylight, 35 mm lens
Kodachrome-25

65

*Droue-s-Drouette,
France
June 1982*
Daylight, 135 mm lens
Kodachrome-64

67

*Malibu, California
February 1983*
Daylight, Flash, 20 mm lens
Kodachrome-25

69

*Pasadena, California
January 1983*
Daylight, 35 mm lens
Kodachrome-64

70

*Les Jolis Vaux,
Bussy le Repos, France, IV
May 1983*
Daylight, Flash, 24 mm lens
Kodachrome-64

71

*Les Jolis Vaux,
Bussy le Repos, France, V
May 1983*
Daylight, Flash, 24 mm lens
Kodachrome-64

73

*Les Jolis Vaux,
Bussy le Repos, France, VI
May 1983*
Daylight, Flash, 24 mm lens
Kodachrome-64

74

*Les Jolis Vaux,
Bussy le Repos, France, VII
May 1983*
Flash, 35 mm lens
Kodachrome-25

75

*Les Jolis Vaux,
Bussy le Repos, France, VIII
May 1983*
Flash, 35 mm lens
Kodachrome-25

76

*Nemours, France, III
April 1983*
Flash, 28 mm lens
Kodachrome-25

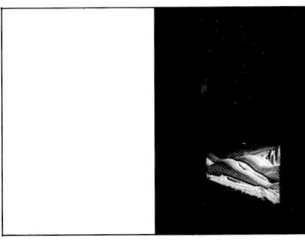

77

*Nemours, France, IV
April 1983*
Flash, 28 mm lens
Kodachrome-25

78

*Los Angeles, California, I
January 1983*
Daylight, 28 mm lens
Kodachrome-64

79

*Los Angeles, California, II
January 1983*
Daylight, 135 mm lens
Kodachrome-64

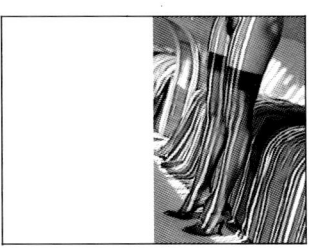
81

Beverly Hills, California
February 1983
Daylight, Flash, 85 mm lens
Kodachrome-25

83

Hollywood, California
December 1982
Daylight, 50 mm lens
Kodachrome-64

85

Los Angeles, California
September 1982
Daylight, Flash, 35 mm lens
Kodachrome-64

86

Long Island, New York, I
May 1980
Daylight, 135 mm lens
Kodachrome-25

87

Long Island, New York, II
May 1980
Daylight, 35 mm lens
Kodachrome-25

The photographs appearing in this book were made using Nikon F-3 cameras, Nikkor lenses, and the Mamiya RZ 67.
Photographs made with flash were made using Balcar equipment.

ACKNOWLEDGMENTS

The author wishes to thank
the following people for their help in making this book possible :
Patrick Robin, Remy Haddad,
Barney Rosset, Charles Brocket, Daniel Filipacchi, Thierry Taittinger,
Manuel Ortiz Juarez, Alain Gres, Danna Hyams, Medwyn Hughes, David Fahey, Ken Marcus,
Christian Langlamet, Sigfried Trichter, Bernie Cornfeld, Pierre Eggermont, Roger Borniche,
Phillip Dixon and Bernard Dannenmuller.

Also his assistants, Lyle Peterzell and Jean-Claude Gay,
his make-up artists Volanta, Paula Owens, Ronnie Spector and Arthur S. Pina.

Special thanks to Alain Viard for his help with the layout,
and to the following for their help and generosity :

Charles Jourdan, Vicky Tiel, Greet *(Paris)*,
The Pleasure Dome *(Los Angeles)* and Lina Lee,
Edwards and Lowe *(Beverly Hills)*.

Also special thanks to all the models who appear in this work, and in particular,
Carin van Eendenburgh, Janie Christensen and Kim Howard.

This book was printed on JOB 200 gram Classic-Brilliant paper,
Printed by Berger-Levrault, Nancy, France in October 1983.
Binding and slip case by Brun, Malesherbes France.

A special edition of this book,
comprised of the first 100 copies printed, signed by the author and numbered,
is available through the publisher.